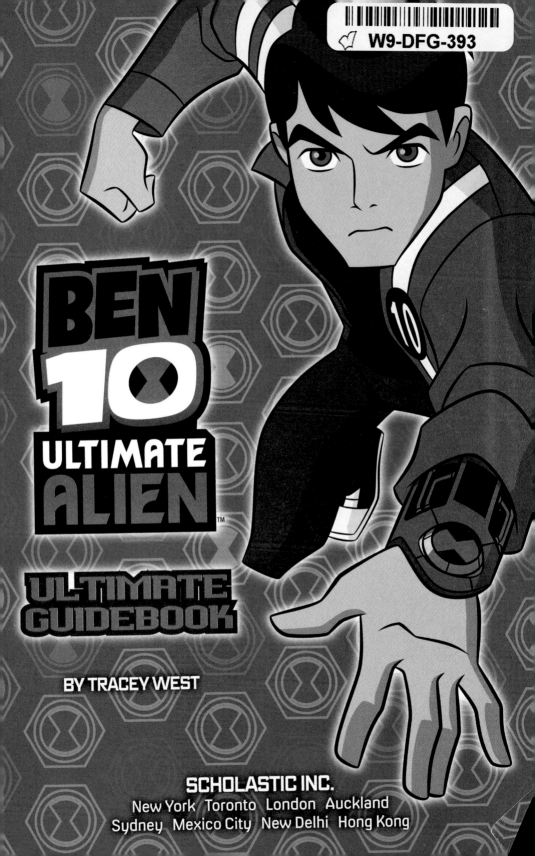

BEN 10 ULTIMATE ALIEN™

ULTIMATE GUIDEBOOK

BY TRACEY WEST

SCHOLASTIC INC.
New York   Toronto   London   Auckland
Sydney   Mexico City   New Delhi   Hong Kong

ISBN 978-0-545-22538-0

CARTOON NETWORK, the logo, Ben 10 Ultimate Alien, and all related characters and elements are trademarks of and © 2010 Cartoon Network.
Published by Scholastic Inc.
SCHOLASTIC and associated logos are trademarks and/or registered trademarks of Scholastic Inc.

12 11 10 9 8 7 6 5 4 3 2 1   10 11 12 13 14 15/0

Printed in the U.S.A.   40
First printing, September 2010

CONTENTS

BEN'S BEGINNINGS

Ben Tennyson was a normal ten-year-old kid — until the day he found the Omnitrix. Once he put on this mysterious alien device, he couldn't take it off. The Omnitrix gave Ben the power to transform into ten different alien life-forms, and whether he wanted to or not, Ben became a superhero.

With the help of his Grandpa Max and cousin Gwen, Ben defeated Vilgax, an alien warlord determined to rule Earth. Ben continued to fight to defend Earth but before he turned eleven he found a way to remove the Omnitrix. His life went back to normal — for awhile.

When Ben was fifteen, an alien race called the HighBreed launched a plan to take over the universe, one planet at a time. Ben strapped the Omnitrix on again and discovered he could transform into new alien forms with it. This time, Ben, Gwen, and Grandpa Max had help from Kevin Levin, a former bad guy with a change of heart.

Ben and his friends saved the universe again. Then Vilgax returned to seek revenge. He kidnapped Gwen and Kevin and then made a trade with Ben: the Omnitrix in return for the lives of his friends. Ben turned over the Omnitrix, but later used a voice command to destroy it so Vilgax couldn't use it.

Now Ben is sixteen and wears a new device — the Ultimatrix. With it, Ben can transform into Ultimate versions of some of his favorite alien forms. But along with his new powers, there's a new villain, Aggregor, who's ready to give Ben his toughest challenge yet. And even though Ben has matured a lot since he inherited the Omnitrix, he still loves to remind everyone that he has, in fact, saved the "whole entire universe" several times — much to the annoyance of Gwen and Kevin!

BEN'S ALIENS

When Ben first got his Omnitrix, it took him awhile to figure out how to use the powers of his ten alien forms. At the touch of a finger, he could access an alien with fiery heat or super speed. But figuring out which power to use wasn't always easy.

As Ben got older, he added new aliens to his arsenal. The more he transformed, the more he knew how to use them.

Now, thanks to the Ultimatrix, Ben can access more aliens than ever before. If he needs to, he can dial up some of his first ten aliens. If he encounters a new life-form, he can scan it and then transform into it right away.

And if Ben needs an extra boost of power, he can Ultimize some of his alien forms: Spidermonkey, Cannonbolt, Echo Echo, Humungousaur, Swampfire, and Big Chill. One click of the Ultimatrix can make him bigger, better, faster, and stronger in seconds. That's a good thing, because Ben is about to face his ultimate enemy!

BEN

Ben Tennyson has changed a lot in the last six years. He used to rush into battle without thinking. He wasn't always nice to his cousin Gwen. Sometimes, it seemed like he didn't take his position as the owner of the Omnitrix seriously.

Now that he's sixteen, Ben still has a fiery spirit, but he's got it under control. He uses strategy in battle, and he doesn't give

SKILLS AND STRENGTHS:

- With the Ultimatrix, Ben has the ability to transform into aliens from all over the universe, each one with its own unique powers.

- Good problem solver

- Never gives up

LIKES:

- Monster movies

- Hanging out at Mr. Smoothy

- Video games (especially "Sumo Slammers")

DISLIKES:

- Riding in the passenger seat

- Aliens who want to rule the universe

- When the Ultimatrix won't work

Gwen such a hard time. And after saving the world more than once, he knows just how serious things can get.

Through it all, Ben has had a good heart. He's a loyal friend and will fight to defend what's right, no matter what the cost.

But now Ben is facing a new kind of challenge: fame. He gets recognized wherever he goes. Mr. Smoothy even has drinks named after each of his alien forms! Ben actually likes his new-found fame, but Gwen and Kevin are worried that his head is getting bigger than Brain-Storm's crablike cranium. Will Ben's own ego end up being his greatest enemy?

THE ULTIMATRIX

Ben's new Omnitrix allows him to Ultimize some of his alien forms, giving them increased powers. However, when Ben uses the Ultimizing function, it drains more power from the Ultimatrix than normal. He's got to be careful not to overuse it.

Ben's original Omnitrix was created by Azmuth, a brilliant Galvan scientist. However, Albedo, Azmuth's former assistant, created the Ultimatrix. Albedo stole parts from Azmuth's lab, hoping to create his own Omnitrix — the result was the Ultimatrix. But it didn't work right away. Albedo had tried to steal the Omnitrix once before, and Azmuth left him trapped in Ben's form as punishment.

As "Negative Ben," Albedo built the Ultimatrix. But when he couldn't access all of the alien forms inside it, he teamed with Vilgax to steal Ben's Omnitrix again so he could reset the Ultimatrix. But Vilgax turned on Negative Ben. In the end, Ben freed Negative Ben — in exchange for the Ultimatrix.

AMPFIBIAN

SPECIES: AMPERI

SKILLS AND STRENGTHS:

- Fires electric bolts from his hands
- Reads minds
- Travels through electrical wires
- Steals power from electric lines
- Transforms into an electron energy being to avoid capture

WEAKNESS:

- Water

Amperi are masters of the electromagnetic spectrum, and they can manipulate electricity in all of its forms. Ben copied Amperi DNA into the Ultimatrix when he scanned Ra'ad, one of the aliens abducted by Aggregor.

When Ben first transformed, Ra'ad was hiding in the Ultimatrix to avoid Aggregor. In his energy form, he was able to merge with Ben's body, nearly destroying Ben's life-force. Kevin reactivated the Ultimatrix just in time to set Ben free.

Ampfibian just might be one of Ben's most powerful forms, but he's still getting used to this new form. Maybe one day he'll be shocked to learn all that Ampfibian can do!

ARMODRILLO

SKILLS AND STRENGTHS:

- Can drill deep underground at fast speed
- Creates tremors to knock opponents off their feet
- Has a powerful jackhammer punch that literally shakes things up!

Ben acquired this new alien form after he scanned the DNA of Andreas, one of the aliens kidnapped by Aggregor. It's easy to understand why Aggregor wanted to absorb the power of Andreas. This alien form is not only big and strong, but he can quickly and easily drill through solid rock.

When two Forever Knights attacked Ben, he transformed into Armodrillo for the first time. He quickly drilled underground to avoid the knights' energy swords. As the puzzled knights wondered where he had gone, he dug a hole right underneath them that swallowed them up.

BIG CHILL

SPECIES: NECROFRIGGIAN

This spectrelike alien looks like he belongs in a haunted house, but Big Chill is from an icy planet called Kylmyys. Ben transforms into Big Chill whenever he needs to stop his enemies in their tracks, fast. Big Chill can freeze an opponent with one blast of his sub-zero breath.

SKILLS AND STRENGTHS:

- Flight
- Ice-Cold Breath
- Mistlike body can pass through solid matter

ULTIMATE BIG CHILL

SPECIES: NECROFRIGGIAN

Ultimate Big Chill combines the destructive power of fire with the freezing power of ice. Ben first transformed into Ultimate Big Chill to battle Vulkanus. One blast of Ultimate Big Chill's breath melted this alien's shell of armor.

Ben has also used this form to create a wall of ice between himself and a crowd of crazed teenage fans. Now that's cold!

SKILLS AND STRENGTHS:

• Fiery breath so cold that it burns

• Creates a wall of ice-cold flame that can trap more than one enemy

• Can make snow fall on a summer day

BRAIN STORM

SPECIES: CEREBROCRUSTACEAN

When Ben transformed into Brain Storm to battle Aggregor, he was overconfident.

"You'll find that challenging an intellectually superior foe often leads to humiliation," Brain Storm told Aggregor smugly.

But Brain Storm was in for a shock—literally—when Aggregor attacked him with his Shock Staff. The weapon was specially calibrated to cause damage to electromagnetic species. Brain Storm nearly died, but Ra'ad turned himself over to Aggregor to save Ben's life.

SKILLS AND STRENGTHS:

- Super-enhanced brainpower
- Zaps opponents with highly charged lightning bolts
- Hard exoskeleton protects him from attacks
- Projects protective force fields

CANNONBOLT

SPECIES: ARBURIAN PELAROTA

SKILLS AND STRENGTHS

- Rolls into a ball to flatten attackers
- Hard shell is impervious to most damage
- Able to contain others inside his shell

Ben transforms into Cannonbolt when he needs to knock down foes like bowling pins. But this alien is more than just a living bowling ball. He's got other abilities, too.

When radioactive P'Andor was on the loose, Kevin and Ben knew they had to somehow contain him. Ben transformed into Cannonbolt, who opened up his form and pulled Kevin, P'Andor, and P'Andor's armor inside. Kevin touched the armor and then morphed the metal around P'Andor. Cannonbolt exploded open, shooting out Kevin and a safely contained P'Andor. Nice trick!

ULTIMATE CANNONBOLT

SPECIES: ARBURIAN PELAROTA

SKILLS AND STRENGTHS

- Metallic armor exterior is even stronger than his original form.

- Spikes add extra power to attacks.

In his Ultimate form, Cannonbolt has sharp spikes that protrude from his armor. When he is in ball form, he resembles a spiked mace, a medieval weapon used by knights. Knights used the spiked mace to crush an opponent's armor — just like Ultimate Cannonbolt uses them to crush his enemies.

ECHO ECHO

SPECIES: SONOROSIAN

Sometimes it takes more than one alien to take on an army of foes. That's when Ben transforms into Echo Echo, the tough little alien that can make an endless amount of clones.

Once, Ben figured out that he could use Echo Echo to be in three places at once. First, he transformed into Echo Echo. Then, he made two clones. All three Echo Echo used their Omnitrix to turn back into Ben. One Ben stayed to watch Julie's tennis match, one Ben went with Kevin to fight the Forever Knights, and the third caught the premiere of the *Sumo Slammers* movie.

There was one problem — none of the three Bens was the complete package. Things just didn't work out. He defeated the Forever Knights, but he missed the end of the movie and got into hot water with Julie. In this case, three Bens were definitely *not* better than one.

SKILLS AND STRENGTHS

- Creates multiple duplicates of himself
- Emits sonic wave blasts strong enough to shatter steel
- Uses echolocation to locate objects or navigate in the dark

ULTIMATE ECHO ECHO

SPECIES: SONOROSIAN

When Aggregor was trying to find the four pieces of the Map of Infinity, Ben, Gwen, and Kevin tried to beat him to it. The first piece was kept in a temple on the planet Kylmyys. One half of the planet is as hot as the sun; the other half is a frozen wasteland. The piece of the map was stored in a temple in a neutral zone between the hot and cold sides.

The guardians of the temple, Necrofriggians, didn't want to give the piece of the map to Ben and trapped him, Gwen, and Kevin in a block of ice. They needed to blast their way out — without blowing themselves up in the bargain. So Ben transformed into Ultimate Echo Echo, who shattered the ice with one big sonic blast.

SKILLS
AND
STRENGTHS

•Floating amps detach from his body to deliver a precise sonic blast. A mild blast from one of the amps can cause a life-form to pass out briefly without harming the life-form.

FOUR ARMS

SPECIES: TETRAMAND

SKILLS AND STRENGTHS:

- Packs a powerful punch
- "The Big Smack," a move that causes shockwaves when he stomps on the ground or claps his hands together
- Leaps great distances with his muscular legs

WEAKNESS

- His bulk and strength cause him to lose agility and speed

When Ben was ten, he used Four Arms a lot in battle. That's because this tough alien has a straightforward battle style: punch first, ask questions later. Many foes were taken down by the raw power of this twelve-foot-tall tower of terror.

As he got older, Ben turned to new alien forms when he needed muscle power. But he was happy to find he could dial up Four Arms again with his new Ultimatrix. When Ben faced the villain Ssserpent, he used Four Arms to take down the alien snake.

GOOP

SPECIES: POLYMORPH

SKILLS AND STRENGTHS:

- Changes into any shape
- Secretes a powerful acid he can shoot out at opponents
- If attacked, he can put himself back together

This 200-pound ball of slime is controlled by the spaceshiplike device that hovers above his head. Ben will often transform into Goop when he needs to get into a tight space. Goop can slip under a door and then reform into a humanoid shape. When the Forever Knights imprisoned Ben, Gwen, and Kevin, it was Goop who led the breakout.

HUMUNGOUSAUR

SPECIES: VAXASAURIAN

SKILLS AND STRENGTHS:

- Super strength
- Grows up to sixty feet tall at will
- Lashes out with his long tail

WEAKNESS

- Electricity

When Ben is in big trouble, he transforms into his biggest alien, Humungousaur. This dinosaurlike alien from the planet Terradino is powerful enough to smash a house with one blow. Humungousaur has put a quick end to many of Ben's battles.

Humungousaur has used his strength in all kinds of situations. In order to absorb the powers of five kidnapped aliens, Aggregor used the time portal created by Paradox. The time portal is powered by an entropy pump. If it ever overloads, it would destroy reality for a distance of several light-years.

Ben couldn't stop Aggregor in time, and the energy in the entropy pump built to a dangerous level. He first transformed into Nanomech, but the tiny alien couldn't turn off the time portal. So Ben went in another direction and became Humungousaur. It took every ounce of strength he had, but Humungousaur smashed the time portal and saved the day.

ULTIMATE HUMUNGOUSAUR

SPECIES: VAXASAURIAN

What's bigger and more powerful than Humungousaur? Its Ultimate form, of course! Ultimate Humungousaur is a one-man battle machine. He's covered with armor and spikes to fend off attacks, and he's got super strength and built-in weapons to take down his enemies.

Ben first used Ultimate Humungousaur when he battled P'Andor, the radioactive alien who escaped from Aggregor. He, Gwen, and Kevin tracked P'Andor to an underground mine, where P'Andor stole an industrial drill machine.

During the brawl, the mine collapsed. Luckily, Ben had already transformed into Ultimate Humungousaur. The mighty beast held up the roof of the collapsed mine with his bare hands!

SKILLS AND STRENGTHS:

- Extra muscles give Ultimate Humungousaur even more strength than his regular form
- Heavy, plated scales protect his body like armor
- Spikes on upper body and spiked ball on end of tail can be used both offensively and defensively
- Shoots missiles at enemies with built-in bio-cannons

JET RAY

SPECIES: AEROPHIBIAN

There's no point in trying to make a quick getaway if you're running away from Ben. He'll transform into Jet Ray and track you down in seconds.

The first time Ben faced the Stalker, the out-of-control robot went after an innocent family driving by in a minivan. Ben transformed into Jet Ray to stop the Stalker before the family was harmed. Jet Ray fired a series of powerful neuro-blasts to try to take down the robot. But the Stalker was armed with a giant parabolic mirror.

Jet Ray's neuro-blasts hit the mirror and then bounced off, striking Jet Ray. The super-fast alien was knocked down by his own attack! The Stalker got away — but not for long.

SKILLS AND STRENGTHS:

• Flies at several times the speed of sound

• Can survive in both air and water

• Can maneuver easily around obstacles while flying at top speeds

• Shoots neuro-blasts from his eyes and tail

LODESTAR

SPECIES: ELECRONIA

After Ben stopped the HighBreed from taking over Earth, he discovered that the Omnitrix was programmed with ten new aliens. The first one he transformed into was Lodestar, an Elecronian from the planet Electront. The inhabitants of this desert planet all have the ability to control magnetic fields.

Lodestar's natural magnetism came in handy when Ben was fighting King Urien, the leader of the Forever Knights. Urien was about to crush Ben with a fistful of ancient battle armor when Ben transformed into Lodestar. First, Lodestar used magnetism to stop the metal fist in midair. Then he hurled two magnetic beams at the armor, ripping it off of King Urien piece by piece.

SKILLS AND STRENGTHS:
- Controls magnetic fields
- Attracts and repels magnetic objects
- If his body gets damaged, the magnetic pieces will re-form

NANOMECH

SPECIES: CURRENTLY UNKNOWN

Half of Nanomech's DNA comes from an alien race of tiny, living computer chips that once tried to take over Earth. Plumber Victor Validus saw the dangers early, but when the Plumbers prohibited him from studying the chips, Victor stole them and left to do his own research.

Victor was right about the chips, but he never imagined how dangerous they could really be. The queen of the alien race took up residence in Victor's brain, and he began producing millions of chips — enough to infect everyone on Earth, turning them into zombies.

The only way Ben could fight the chips was to become one of them. He scanned their DNA into the Omnitrix, which then fused Ben's DNA with the alien race. The half-human, half-chip Nanomech flew inside Victor's brain and beat the queen in a one-on-one battle. Once the queen died, the chips were no longer active.

Ben often finds that Nanomech's small size comes in handy. When Will Harangue programmed his robot, the Stalker, to counter all of Ben's alien forms, he missed Nanomech. In the end, only the tiny alien could take down the giant killer robot.

SKILLS AND STRENGTHS:

• Can shrink to the size of an atom

• Flies

• Blasts opponents with powerful jolts of electricity

RATH

SPECIES: APPOPLEXIAN

When you shoot Rath, it just makes Rath mad!"

That's what Rath told the Forever Knights when they attacked him, but the Knights didn't listen. In retaliation, Rath ripped up their armored tank into pieces with his bare hands.

Rath has a short temper and the personality of a flashy professional wrestler. When he gets angry, this powerhouse becomes a raging vehicle of destruction. If you're in his path, the best thing to do is get out of his way!

SKILLS AND STRENGTHS:

- Super strength that increases when he gets angry
- Energy blasts can't damage him — he's hard to take down

SPIDERMONKEY

SPECIES: ARACHNICHIMP

Spidermonkey has a lot of energy, but sometimes Ben has a tendency to monkey around when he's in this alien form. When the Forever Knights attacked Mr. Smoothy, Ben transformed into Spidermonkey to stop them. The crowds of kids there waved and cheered, and Spidermonkey got distracted. He waved back, putting on a show. If Gwen hadn't raised an energy shield for him, the Forever Knights would have blasted him to bits.

SKILLS AND STRENGTHS:

- Superior agility
- Shoots webs out of his tail to trap foes
- Able to walk up walls

ULTIMATE SPIDERMONKEY

SPECIES: ARACHNICHIMP

Ultimate Spidermonkey looks more like Ultimate Spidergorilla. He's got four muscular gorilla limbs and four spiderlike legs.

When Spidermonkey was battling Bivalvan, the giant clam sent him flying with a powerful water blast. Ben transformed into Ultimate Spidermonkey, and then the fight was really on. Bivalvan and Ultimate Spidermonkey traded punches. After Bivalvan was weakened, Ultimate Spidermonkey trapped him in a thick web cocoon.

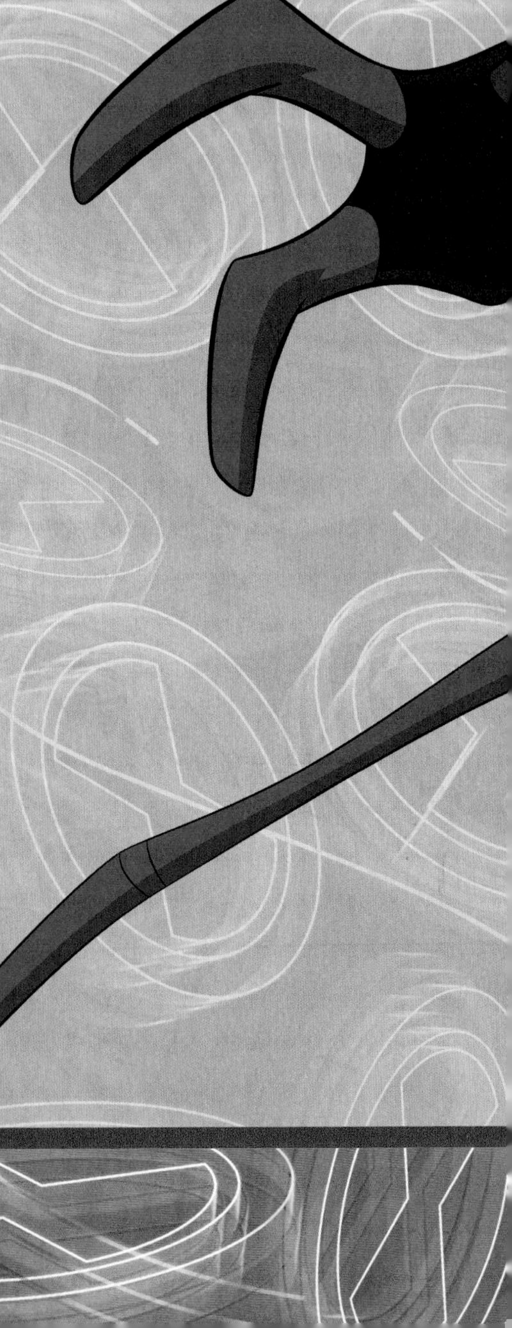

SKILLS AND STRENGTHS:

- Superior strength
- Shoots ultra-thick webbing from his mouth

SWAMPFIRE

SPECIES: METHANOSIAN

Swampfire looks like a living plant and smells like a drawer full of dirty socks. But he's one of Ben's most versatile forms. Not only can Swampfire deliver fiery attacks, but he can take a lot of damage. If he loses an arm or leg in battle he can grow a new one right away.

Swampfire comes from the planet Methanos, a swampy planet bathed in stinky methane gas. The atmosphere would be toxic to humans, but Methanosians thrive here. It's this methane gas that gives Swampfire his fire power.

SKILLS AND STRENGTHS:

- Shoots flames from his hands
- Regenerates damaged body parts
- Objects pass harmlessly through his body
- Controls plants with the gas he emits from his body

ULTIMATE SWAMPFIRE

SPECIES: METHANOSIAN

He's bulkier and smellier than Swampfire, and thanks to the blue sacs of napalm on his body, Ultimate Swampfire is a lot more dangerous.

Ben first transformed into Ultimate Swampfire during a battle with Aggregor. The evil alien was holding five kidnapped aliens inside the Los Soledad military base so he could drain their powers. He guarded the base with an army of killer robots.

Ultimate Swampfire blasted the robots with a barrage of napalm bombs. They melted one by one.

SKILLS AND STRENGTHS:

- Organic napalm sacs growing from his body can be hurled like bombs at an enemy
- Shoots super-powerful flames from his hands like twin flame-throwers

TERRASPIN

SPECIES: CURRENTLY UNKNOWN

SKILLS AND STRENGTHS:

•When Terraspin retracts his head inside his shell, a propeller emerges that allows him to spin with amazing speed, propelling himself at his enemies like a missile

•Hard shell provides excellent defense

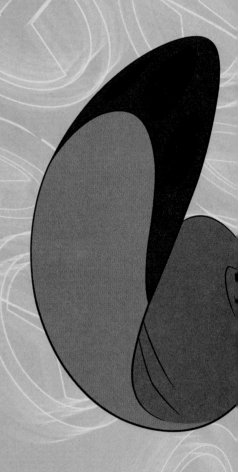

Ben gained the form of Terraspin when he scanned the DNA of Galapagus, one of the five aliens kidnapped by Aggregor. Galapagus wasn't much of a fighter, but Ben quickly figured out how to use the alien's abilities to his advantage.

When Ben, Gwen, and Kevin were investigating a crashed alien ship, the ship's ten-foot-tall robot guard attacked. Terraspin slammed into the robot, then grabbed it and began to spin around and around. The sheer force tore the robot into pieces.

UPCHUCK

SPECIES: GOURMAND

All right — the ability to attack your enemies with super-puke is pretty gross as far as powers go. But think about it. Upchuck can take a weapon that's supposed to hurt him and turn it against his opponent. As much as Ben hates turning into Upchuck, sometimes this alien form is the only one that will do the trick!

SKILLS AND STRENGTHS:

- Can eat and digest almost anything with his four stretchable stomachs
- Transforms what he eats into explosives or acid to shoot at enemies
- Latches onto objects with his four sticky tongues

WEAKNESS

- Upchuck cannot digest human food or other organic matter (such as people)

WAY BIG

SPECIES: TO'KUSTAR

SKILLS AND STRENGTHS:

- Way Big is Ben's largest alien, reaching nearly 100 feet — the size of a small skyscraper
- Incredible strength
- Nearly invulnerable

Way Big doesn't have a planet to call home; He was created as an anomaly during a cosmic storm. Azmuth, the creator of the Omnitrix, unlocked this form for Ben so he could defeat Vilgax and his army. Only Way Big has what it takes to take on an entire army by himself.

Ben doesn't use Way Big often, but he did transform into the giant alien when talk show host Will Harangue sent the Stalker robot after Ben. Once Ben won the battle, Way Big crushed the robot into a ball with his bare hands — and then lobbed it at Harangue's car.

WATERHAZARD

WaterHazard may look like he couldn't survive outside of water, but don't be fooled — this alien is a tough customer. His outer armor is invulnerable, and he's got some pretty sweet offensive moves, too.

Ben scanned the DNA of Bivalvan, one of the five aliens kidnapped by Aggregor, to obtain his WaterHazard form.

SKILLS AND STRENGTHS:

- Tough outer armor
- Blasts opponents with powerful water jets

BEN'S TEAM

Ben might have an army of aliens at his disposal thanks to his Ultimatrix, but he still can't save the universe without help from his friends and family. Luckily, Ben has plenty of people he can count on.

When he was ten, his Grandpa Max guided him and his cousin Gwen on their alien-fighting missions. When he turned fifteen, former-enemy-turned-friend Kevin Levin joined the team.

In this section, you'll meet the characters who've helped Ben with advice, know-how, support, and sheer muscle power. Some of them are by his side all the time, and some only appear when they're needed. But all of them are good guys at heart.

GWEN TENNYSON

SKILLS AND STRENGTHS:

- Able to produce powerful energy blasts
- Can track the energy field of living beings
- Expert martial artist
- Working knowledge of magic spells
- Reads auras to determine if a person is lying

LIKES:

- Shopping with Julie
- Kevin (when he's not being a jerk)

DISLIKES:

- Aliens that can block her energy blasts
- Kevin (when he's being a jerk)

Ben's cousin Gwen has been with him from the beginning. When Kevin and Ben get hot-headed, Gwen's the one who keeps things focused. She's the most thoughtful member of the team, and she values a good strategy over an impulsive attack.

Ben and Gwen's grandmother is an Anodite alien, and Gwen was born with a big dose of alien DNA. Anodites are beings made of pure energy, and it's the alien part of her that gives her the ability to create and manipulate energy. If Gwen ever gets tired of being human, she can go to Anodyne and transform into a pure energy being, shedding her human form forever.

Luckily, Gwen likes being human, and she's focused on helping her teammates fight whatever alien danger comes their way. That's good for Ben, because Gwen's quick thinking and energy shields have saved his life more than a few times.

KEVIN E. LEVIN

SKILLS AND STRENGTHS:

- Able to transform into any metal he touches
- Familiar with alien technology from all over the universe
- Capable of fixing just about any vehicle

LIKES:

- Working at the Bellwood Auto Shop fixing up his muscle car
- Fast food
- Gwen

DISLIKES:

- Authority

ike Gwen, Kevin is part alien. He's an Osmosian on his father's side. His dad was a Plumber, but he died when Kevin was young.

After his father died, Kevin went down a dark path. He tried to use his powers to take over the Earth, but ended up in the Null Void thanks to Ben, Gwen, and Grandpa Max.

After he escaped from the Null Void, Kevin finally started to get things right. Sure, he was a dealer of alien technology for awhile, but he stopped that when he began helping Ben and Gwen fight the HighBreed, an alien race intent on taking over Earth.

These days Kevin uses his skills with alien technology to customize the vehicles he and the team use to pursue alien bad guys. Kevin's always around when Ben needs him, and he never backs down from a challenge. But what Kevin might be most proud of is that he now wears a Plumbers' badge — just like his dad once did.

SANDRA AND KARL TENNYSON

Ben's parents are an easygoing couple who love nature. But when they discovered that their son had been fighting aliens for years without their knowledge, they got tough.

Ben was grounded from saving the world — no cell phone, no computer, and above all, no using the Omnitrix. Sandra was especially worried about Ben's safety. And Karl never liked the secret life led by his father, Max. He didn't want Ben keeping secrets, either.

Then Kevin was locked in a losing battle with a HighBreed, and Ben had to make a tough choice between obeying his parents and saving his friend. Ben chose to save Kevin, and Sandra and Karl realized that what Ben was doing was important. Now they let Ben fight the alien menace whenever he wants — as long as he's home at a reasonable hour and remembers to wear a jacket when it's chilly out.

KEN TENNYSON

Gwen and Ben always looked up to Gwen's older brother, Ken. Ken took Ben to his first soccer game. He snuck Gwen and her friends backstage when his band played. Ken was a typical college student with a junky car and a pretty normal life. He had no idea his little sister and cousin were fighting evil aliens.

Then Ken's car broke down in the wrong part of town one day. DNAliens captured him and used him as bait to lure Grandpa Max to their hideout. They used a parasite called a Xenocite to turn Ken into a hideous DNAlien.

With the help of Ben, Gwen, and Kevin, Grandpa Max rescued Ken. Ben used the Omnitrix to transform Ken into a human again. Now Ken knows his family's secret — as well as the secret threat that could destroy all of humankind.

VERDONA

Verdona is Ben and Gwen's grandmother. She may look like a sweet lady with white hair, but that's not her true form. She's really an Anodite alien from the planet Anodyne — a being of pure energy. Anodites are free spirits who can master the manipulation of Manna, life energy.

When Verdona was younger, she fell in love with Max Tennyson and settled down. She's the mother of Ben's dad, Karl, and Gwen's dad, Mike. But she left her Earth family behind long ago to explore her heritage on Anodyne.

Every once in a while, Verdona checks in to see what's happening on Earth. When she discovered that Gwen had inherited her abilities, she wanted Gwen to go back to Anodyne with her, leaving her human body behind. Gwen wanted to stay on Earth, but Verdona wouldn't take no for an answer. Spidermonkey and Kevin battled Verdona until she changed her mind. She left Earth peacefully, but promised to drop in again to see how Gwen was doing.

COOPER

ooper is a shy, quiet kid who rarely leaves his basement computer lab. But Cooper doesn't spend all of his time on massive multiplayer online role-playing games. He's got a special talent. He's a techno-path, which means he can communicate with and understand technology — including alien technology.

That's exactly why the HighBreed aliens want Cooper. They sent DNAliens to capture Cooper. Then they forced him to create their secret alien technology. Cooper didn't know exactly what he was making, but he was pretty sure it was going to be used for sinister purposes.

Ben, Gwen, and Kevin saved Cooper from the aliens, but they can't save him from the huge crush he has on Gwen. His yen for Gwen is one big reason he's sure to help Ben and his friends save the world if he's ever needed again.

JULIE YAMAMOTO

SKILLS AND STRENGTHS:
- Competitive tennis player

LIKES:
- Her alien pet, Ship
- Monster movies
- Amusement park rides

Julie likes monsters, and aliens as much as Ben does — which is pretty much a requirement if you want to be Ben's girlfriend. Julie's always eager to go on missions with Ben, Gwen, and Kevin. She'll jump in whenever she's needed.

It also helps that Ship, a Mechomorph alien, likes Julie and acts as her part-time pet. Ship can absorb any type of technology and transform into it, whether it's a weapon or a super-charged spaceship.

But being a hero's girlfriend isn't easy, especially when that hero is an easily distracted teenager like Ben. He's always going off without warning to fight some kind of an emergen-cy, and once he got into trouble when he tried to skip out on Julie's first big tennis match. Only time will tell if Julie and Ben will stay together for the long run.

JT AND CASH

If you know JT and Cash, you're probably wondering why these teens are lumped in with the good guys. For years, these bullies made Ben's life miserable in school. And when Cash got hold of some alien technology, he briefly terrorized Bellwood as a powerful robot.

After that incident, both boys came to realize that Ben was an okay guy — one who had saved the people of Bellwood over and over again. They stopped bullying him and actually started being helpful — as helpful as a couple of not-so-bright dudes can be, anyway.

When JT and Cash started a webcast about Ben, they made it seem like they were the brains of the operation. Ben agreed to go along with the filming of their show for a cut of the profits. Things got serious when the villain Psyphon came to Earth to seek revenge on Ben. In the end, JT and Cash actually saved Ben's life by activating an alien weapon—but nobody saw them. They thought the boys were lying again. For now, only JT and Cash know how brave they can really be.

JIMMY JONES

SKILLS AND STRENGTHS:
•Runs a website about Ben and his alien forms

LIKES:
•Ben Tennyson; Jimmy is his #1 fan

DISLIKES:
•When his mom makes him go to gymnastics class

Ben was able to keep his identity as an alien-fighting hero a secret for years. Then one day, a website appeared with video clips of Ben in a bunch of different battles.

Ben, Kevin, and Gwen tracked the website to a house in Bellwood. They expected to find an evil mastermind behind the site. Instead, they found ten-year-old Jimmy — Ben's biggest fan.

Jimmy started collecting video footage of alien sightings around Bellwood. He soon noticed the Omnitrix symbol on all of them. It wasn't too long before he put the pieces together and figured out that Ben was able to transform.

Jimmy thought he was doing Ben a favor by making him famous. He didn't realize that Ben would be swarmed by paparazzi and fans wherever he went, making it difficult for Ben to keep up his fight against bad guys. The website might be a nuisance, but it's helpful, too. If a new alien form is invading Earth, Jimmy's usually the first one to notice.

GRANDPA MAX

When he was younger, Grandpa Max spent a lot of time on the field fighting aliens face to face. These days, he spends most of his time in the Plumbers secret headquarters in Bellwood, tracking alien activity around the universe.

That doesn't mean Grandpa Max is out of action. When things get tough, he's right there on the front lines. When the Plumbers tracked down Aggregor's spaceship, Grandpa Max went along with Ben, Kevin, and Gwen to try to capture the villain and free the kidnapped aliens. He blasted Aggregor's robots with the skill of a seasoned pro.

SKILLS AND STRENGTHS:

- Expert knowledge of alien life-forms and technology
- Excellent leader
- Trained Plumber
- Packs a mean punch

LIKES:

- Really gross food
- Hawaiian shirts

ALSO KNOWN AS:

- The "Wrench," after he ended up in the Null Void and saved this extradimensional prison from a villain named D'Void.

SHIP

Ship is a Mechomorph from the moon Galvan B. Like the rest of his kind, Ship's body is made up entirely of living nanotechnology. That means he can absorb any technology and transform into it.

Most Mechomorphs are humanoid, but Ship is more like a pet. He came to Earth in the body of a Mechomorph space pilot. When the pilot's ship crashed, he sent out a part of his body — Ship — to get help. Ship sought out Ben, who was on a date with Julie at the time. Humungousaur saved the ship, and the pilot flew back home, leaving Ship behind. Since then, Ship has remained fond of Julie, and he visits her from time to time.

Ship once got into trouble when the Forever Knights kidnapped him and turned him into an Antarian Obliterator, a spaceship with awesome powers of destruction. Kevin and his friends helped Ship escape — and now Ship can transform into the gunship whenever he wants to.

PARADOX

When Paradox shows up, you know things are going to get interesting. This time-traveling scientist only appears when the universe is in terrible danger. Now he's back to warn Ben that Aggregor has the power to destroy the entire known universe if he's not stopped.

His own adventure began in the 1950s when he was a scientist working at Los Soledad military base. He built a time portal that actually worked — but when it malfunctioned, he became trapped in time and space for eons.

Paradox knows what the future holds, but he also knows that the fabric of space and time is always changing. He always gives Ben just enough information to save the day — but in the end, it's up to Ben to do it.

MAGISTER PRIOR GILHIL

Gilhil is a busy officer with more than three hundred planets under his charge. He's a big fan of law and order, and he really hates rule-breakers. When he got a tip that Ben, Gwen, and Kevin were "impersonating" Plumbers, he traveled to Earth to put them all under arrest.

Magister Gilhil took away Kevin's Plumbers' badge and left the friends with a stern warning to stop impersonating officers of the law. He wasn't gone for long when a HighBreed attacked, forcing Ben, Gwen, and Kevin to use their powers to defend themselves. Gilhil arrived on the scene, ready to send them all to the Null Void for harming a "defenseless" High-Breed.

When the truth came out — that villain Darkstar was trying to frame his enemies — Gilhil realized that Ben and his friends were doing important work. Instead of arresting them, he drafted them as Plumbers in the quadrant.

AZMUTH

The inventor of the Omnitrix, Azmuth is a scientist from the planet Galvan Prime. He created the Omnitrix for Grandpa Max, one of the greatest Plumbers in the universe. When it accidentally ended up on Ben's wrist, Azmuth wasn't pleased. He knows that Ben is doing a good job, but Azmuth always keeps an eye on him.

Azmuth was working on a new, improved device called the Ultimatrix when it was stolen by his old assisant, Albedo. Ben got the device back from Albedo and decided to wear it after the Omnitrix was destroyed. That has Azmuth worried. The Ultimatrix wasn't finished when it was stolen, and he's sure something will go wrong. But he still turns to Ben when he knows the universe is in trouble — and Ben is the only one who can save it.

THE PLUMBERS

The Plumbers are a lot like the police: they catch bad guys and carry badges. But the bad guys they catch are from other planets, and the weapons they use to catch them are made from alien tech.

On Earth, the Plumbers are a secret government organization, but there are Plumbers in every galaxy. Their main goal is to keep peace in the universe,

and they do a pretty good job of it. They've captured hundreds of criminals in their blue en-

ergy cuffs and zapped them into the Null Void, an extradimensional prison.

But the Plumbers may have met their match in Aggregor. First, Aggregor kidnapped five aliens from the far corners of the universe. The aliens escaped and landed on Earth. Ben and his friends located them one by one and entrusted them with the Plumbers to get them home safely.

But one by one, Aggregor attacked the Plumbers' ships and

recaptured the five aliens. That was a dark time for the Plumbers. If the Plumbers can't keep the universe safe, then who can?

Luckily, Ben, Kevin, and Gwen all carry Plumbers' badges. They might be new at the job, but they're a real credit to the force.

PLUMBERS HQ

On Earth, the Plumbers have a secret headquarters in the basement of the Bellwood Auto Shop. That's usually where you'll find Grandpa Max, munching on a squid sandwich and checking the monitors for any illegal alien activity.

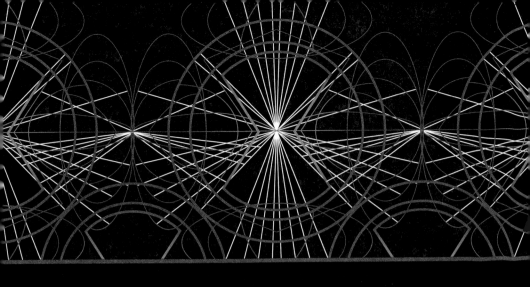

THE RISE OF AGGREGOR

It all started with the mysterious disappearance of five aliens from all over the universe. They were snatched from such remote places that the Plumbers didn't even know there was a problem.

The aliens managed to escape, but crash-landed on Earth. Ben and his friends encountered them one by one and the plot began to unfold: They were kidnapped by a power-hungry alien, Aggregor, so he could absorb all of their powers. Aggregor wanted to become a superbeing in order to achieve his goal: ultimate domination of the universe.

AGGREGOR

Aggregor is an Osmosian, like Kevin. Osmosians can absorb matter, energy, or the powers of any living creature. But while Kevin mostly uses his powers to absorb things like steel and stone, Aggregor had more sinister plans for his powers. He used the menacing energy of his Shock Staff to kidnap five aliens. Then he absorbed them to increase his own strength, skill, and invulnerability.

Once he absorbed the five aliens, Aggregor became Ultimate Aggregor. This seemingly invincible villain had a terrible plan. First, he would steal the four pieces of the Map of Infinity, a complete map of space, time, and alternate dimensions. Once the map was put together, it would lead him to the Forge of Creation at the center of the universe.

"If we don't stop him, the entire universe will tremble at his might," Azmuth warned Ben, Gwen, and Kevin. Ben knew he had to channel all of his strength to fight Aggregor, perhaps his most dangerous foe ever.

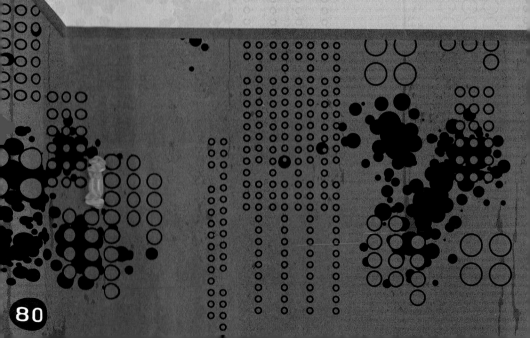

BIVALVAN

Bivalvan was the first of the five kidnapped aliens that Ben encountered. Jimmy Jones spotted the alien first, after fans of his website reported sightings of a strange creature in Florida.

When Ben, Gwen, and Kevin got there, they discovered that Bivalvan was stealing spaceship parts from NASA to repair his own ship. When he wanted to use a nuclear bomb to power his ship, Ben had to stop him to save millions of lives.

Bivalvan blasted Ben with strong jets of water. Ben fought back as Ultimate Spidermonkey, but he couldn't crack Bivalvan's hard shell. It finally took a supersticky web to stop Bivalvan from powering his ship.

Ben turned Bivalvan over to the Plumbers. But instead of a ride home, Bivalvan got kidnapped by Aggregor again. Now the Osmosian was one step closer to his goal. . . .

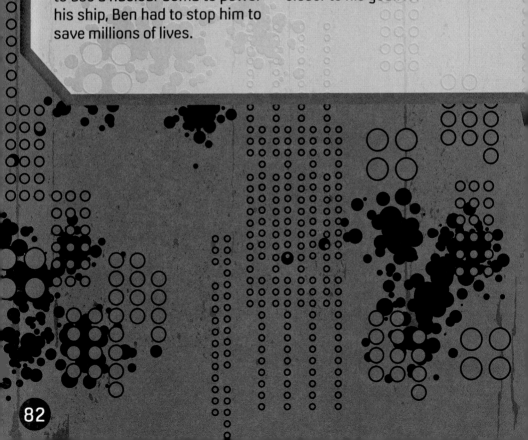

GALAPAGUS

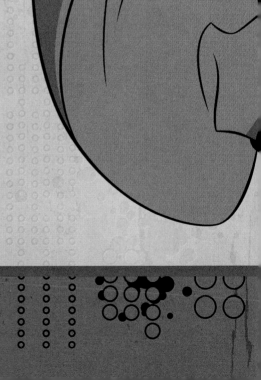

On the peaceful planet of Aldabra, the inhabitants spent their days eating grass, hovering aboveground, and debating philosophy. That's exactly what Galapagus was doing when Aggregor showed up, attacked his friends, and kidnapped him.

Galapagus had never seen a spaceship before. He'd never had to learn to fight, either. But he quickly learned to use his propeller in his chest to create a whirlwind attack as he and the other kidnapped aliens fought to escape their captor.

After the escape from Aggregor, his ship crashed on Earth. Galapagus had a plan: to find the great Ben Tennyson, the hero celebrated in song and story all over the universe. He decided the best way to get Ben's attention was to rampage through downtown Bellwood. True to his nature, though, Galapagus didn't harm any living beings — although he destroyed several buildings in the process!

P'ANDOR

It was an offer Kevin couldn't refuse — one million dollars, cash, to break open an armored suit to free an alien trapped inside. Kevin transformed his arm into a blade made of Taydenite, the hardest metal in the universe. The armor was just about to crack when Kevin's Plumbers' badge let out a warning: the alien inside was emitting dangerous amounts of radiation.

That alien was P'Andor, one of the aliens kidnapped by Aggregor. Kevin refused to do the job and went to let Ben and Gwen know what happened. In the meantime, P'Andor grew more desperate each moment he spent inside the suit, unable to feed. He kidnapped Kevin, who accidentally cut into his arm. P'Andor was free.

P'Andor started gobbling up electricity like a hungry man at an all-you-can-eat buffet. He was emitting so much radiation it was unsafe to get near him. Ben tried to trick him by transforming into WaterHazard, Bivalvan's form. Then he tried freezing P'Andor in his form as Big Chill. Neither ploy worked.

Then P'Andor snacked on some uranium rods from a nuclear power plant, and the situation became code red. Ben and Kevin had to team up to get P'Andor safely back in his armor. The world was safe from P'Andor, but P'Andor wasn't safe from Aggregor. He was recaptured when Aggregor attacked the Plumbers' spaceship, taking P'Andor back to his home planet.

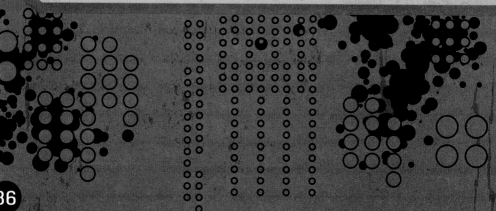

When this mostly gentle giant escaped from Aggregor, he was discovered by another villain, Argit. This porcupine-like alien is a master of shady deals, and when he befriended Andreas, he quickly figured out how to exploit the trusting alien.

Besides being huge and strong, Andreas can walk through solid rock and cause earthquakes. Argit used Andreas to blackmail the Forever Knights: either they gave Argit anything he wanted, or Argit would have Andreas destroy every one of their castles.

For awhile, Argit lived like a king on stolen tacos and smoothies provided by the Knights. That's when Ben, Gwen, and Kevin caught up to him. Then the knights fought back, led by the brave Sir Dagonet. Ben, Gwen, Kevin, and Argit escaped, but Andreas was captured, and scheduled for execution by the alien-hating Forever Knights.

Ben and the others staged a rescue, but the Knights trapped them. Then Sir Dagonet set off a sonic cannon, a weapon with enough power to destroy them all. Andreas grabbed the cannon and drilled deep into the Earth to absorb the explosion — and save his new friend, Argit.

Everyone thought Andreas was gone forever, but he was just buried deep under the rubble. Aggregor found him and brought him onto his spaceship. His collection of super-powers was nearly complete.

While Ben and his friends searched for the escaped aliens, one of them came looking for them. Ra'ad attacked Ben at night, and Ben transformed into Jet Ray to fight him off. At first, it was impossible to do any damage to Ra'ad, who appeared to be made of electricity. But a dunk in the pool took out Ra'ad temporarily.

Why did Ra'ad attack? He knew how Aggregor was finding the escaped aliens — by using Ben's Ultimatrix as a homing device. Ra'ad was determined to destroy the Ultimatrix before Aggregor found him.

Ra'ad damaged the Ultimatrix and vanished just before Aggregor attacked. Ben transformed into an Amperi, the same alien species as Ra'ad, to battle Aggregor. But that wasn't his smartest move. All Aggregor had to do was capture Ben in his Amperi form and his collection would be complete!

Thanks to a teleportation spell of Gwen's, Ben, Kevin, and Gwen escaped. But they didn't realize they brought Ra'ad with them, trapped inside the busted Ultimatrix. He tried to take over Ben in his Amperi body. But Kevin rebooted the Ultimatrix, and Ben and Ra'ad were separated.

Aggregor followed the signal of the Ultimatrix and arrived on the scene. Ben transformed into Brain Storm to battle him. A blow from Aggregor's Shock Staff almost took out Brain Storm for good. Then Aggregor tried to use the Ultimatrix to turn Ben back into an Amperi, nearly killing him.

He almost succeeded when Ra'ad arrived and turned himself over to Aggregor to save Ben. Then he left Ben, determined to find Aggregor and save the five captured aliens, before it was too late for all of them.

ULTIMATE AGGREGGOR

Ben, Gwen, and Kevin fought hard, but they couldn't stop Aggregor from absorbing the energy of the five kidnapped aliens. He became Ultimate Aggregor, a monster with Aggregor's face and the best offensive and defensive parts of the aliens he absorbed.

First, the defense: Thanks to Galapagus, Ultimate Aggregor can't be harmed by energy blasts. Bivalvan's invincible armor protects him from physical attacks.

Then comes the offense: He's got the brute strength of Andreas, the electrocution powers of Ra'ad, and to top it all off, he can use P'Andor's powers to create an explosion with the intensity of a nuclear bomb.

All those powers put together make for one super being — a being capable of destroying the universe, and that's just what Ultimate Aggregor seemed to be trying to do. Fighting Ultimate Aggregor soon proved to be Ben's biggest challenge ever.

MIKE MORNINGSTAR

ith his blond hair and piercing blue eyes, this handsome hunk looks like a movie star. When Ben first met Mike, he thought Mike was another hero like him. Ben and his friends were struggling to save bystanders from a collapsed bridge when Mike flew in, trailing glittery stars behind him. When Ben saw Mike's Plumbers' badge, he was sure Mike was just the person they needed to join their team and save the world.

Mike was the son of a Plumber, and he had amazing powers — but he was no hero. Mike craved power, and the only way he could get it was by draining the energy of unsuspecting teenage girls, turning them into zombies. When he witnessed Gwen's amazing

abilities, he quickly turned on the charm. He knew her strong energy would give him all of the power he wanted.

Mike turned Gwen into a zombie, but she didn't stay that way for long. Gwen fought back and took back her energy. Then the zombie girls got their life force back too. Mike turned into a zombie himself — but that wasn't the end of Mike Morningstar....

Shriveled and weak, Mike Morningstar vowed revenge on Ben and his friends. He donned a mask, put on a new costume, and became the villain Darkstar.

Darkstar was clever. Knowing he was too weak to fight right away, he tried to get Ben, Gwen, and Kevin sent to the Null Void by framing them for a crime. When all three were about to be arrested by Plumber Magister Gilhil, Darkstar swept in and quickly used his Indigo Beams to drain everyone of their power — everyone except Gwen. She gathered a bunch of angry DNAliens with a grudge against Darkstar to join the fight. They defeated Darkstar, and Gilhil took the villain to the Null Void.

Even though Darkstar was a bad guy, Ben knew he needed all of the Plumbers' kids to help when the HighBreed were poised to destroy Earth. So Gwen and Kevin sprang Darkstar from the Null Void. Darkstar came through — but he disappeared before he could be sent back to the Null Void again.

Sevenseven is a bounty hunter from the planet Sotoragg. Under his armor is a creature with a large, gaping mouth filled with sharp teeth.

Five years ago, Ben encountered a Sotoraggian bounty hunter named Sixsix. He first learned about Sevenseven when he kidnapped Princess Attea of the Incursean Empire. Raff, the right-hand man of the empire, told Ben that Sevenseven was the same race as Sixsix, but far more dangerous. "Yeah, eleven more dangerous," Gwen deadpanned.

Sevenseven tried to help Princess Attea overthrow her father's throne, but Swampfire stopped him. Sevenseven's armor cracked, he got one whiff of Swampfire, and then he ran off to wherever it is that bounty hunters hang out.

Dr. Animo was a researcher in veterinary science who once tried to mutate animals in an attempt to take over the world. His evil plans got him sent to the Null Void.

Since he couldn't take over Earth, Dr. Animo tried to take over the Null Void instead. He gained control of the animal-like Null Guardians and began terrorizing the innocent inhabitants of the void. He forced them to mine for Kormite, a powerful stone that he planned to use to break through the impenetrable void. The Kormite also gave him increased power, turning him into the villain known as D'Void.

But D'Void didn't count on Ben finding him in the Null Void. With the help of Grandpa Max and Plumbers' Helpers Manny, Helen, and Pierce, Ben destroyed the Kormite furnace — along with Dr. Animo's hopes of domination.

MORE BAD GUYS

You might think that taking on one all-powerful, insane villain bent on destroying the universe was enough for one hero — but things are never simple when you're Ben Tennyson. Just because Ben's busy doesn't mean other villains are going to take a break.

Most of these villains aren't as dangerous as Aggregor, but they're each dangerous in their own way. To make matters worse, now Ben's got the whole world watching every time he tackles a new bad guy, thanks to Jimmy Jones and his website. That's a lot of pressure when you're trying to save the world and go to high school at the same time.

ARGIT

This alien's quills are super-sharp, but his ability to wheel and deal is even sharper. He's best known as a dealer in alien tech, selling weapons to criminals who'll pay the highest price.

When Argit found Andreas, lost and confused after he escaped Aggregor, he extended a friendly hand to the alien. But Argit had ulterior motives, of course. Armed with several hundred pounds of money-making muscle, Argit attacked the castles of the Forever Knights. Then he made a deal with the alien-hating secret society: Give me whatever I want, and I'll tell Andreas to back off.

Argit was living like a king, but it didn't last. Sir Dagonet of the Forever Knights decided to put an end to Argit's blackmail. In the end, Andreas sacrificed himself to save his new friend, leaving Argit to wheel and deal for another day.

FOREVER KNIGHTS

The Forever Knights have been around for more than a thousand years. Times have changed, but the Knights still wear armor and live in castles.

Still, they're not exactly the knights you read about in tales of yore. For one thing, they've upgraded their weapons to the most sophisticated alien technology. And instead of using their might to save damsels in distress and fight dragons, they've set their sights on a new enemy: aliens.

The problem is, the Forever Knights don't distinguish between bad aliens and good ones. They believe all alien life-forms are a threat to Earth and must be destroyed. Of course, the alien they want to capture the most is Ben.

Ben and the Forever Knights are always at odds. As long as the Knights exist, peace-loving aliens everywhere are in danger.

KING URIEN AND SIR DAGONET

Let's face it, a lot of the Forever Knights are just thugs wearing fancy armor. But some of them stand out.

The Forever Knights have always had a king, and King Urien may just be their most ruthless leader yet. Make him angry, and he'll fry you with an energy blast from his black gauntlet. In his quest for power beyond all reckoning, King Urien stole an ancient necklace from the art museum which transformed into Toltec Battle Armor. The alien armor makes the wearer invincible — unless you're battling Ben and Kevin. Urien learned the hard way not to underestimate his earthly enemies.

While Argit controlled the monstrous alien Andreas, he had the Forever Knights doing his bidding, fetching smoothies and pizza from all over town. Then Sir Dagonet arrived on the scene. This tough warrior wasn't about to answer to Argit. He imprisoned Argit, along with Ben, Gwen, and Kevin, who showed up earlier to save Andreas. Sir Dagonet ordered the execution of them all. Ben, Gwen, and Kevin fought hard, but in the end only a sacrifice by Andreas saved them. Sir Dagonet teleported away, determined to destroy Ben and his friends the next chance he had.

KING URIEN

ROJO

Ben first met this outlaw years ago, when she was a human named Joey who led an all-girl biker gang. These days she's known as Rojo, a cyborg loaded with some serious alien tech.

Ben encountered Rojo and her gang trying to rob a train. He transformed into Rath and battled the three bikers who attacked him with energy weapons. Rojo wrapped an energy chain around Rath's arm and dragged him on her bike. Kevin and Gwen arrived just in time to free Rath. He took down Rojo and her two gang members by destroying their most precious possessions — their wheels.

ZOMBOZO, CHARMCASTER, AND VULKANUS

Ben first encountered — and defeated — these three villains when he was ten years old. Since then, he's thwarted many of their evil plans. Zombozo brought them together to team up and destroy Ben and the entire Tennyson family. But are three villains really better than one?

Part clown, part zombie, Zombozo likes to battle with the dangerous tricks he's got hidden up his sleeve. But his most powerful ability is no laughing matter: He can drain happiness and energy from others and then feed on it.

In the past, Charmcaster's ability to use magic was superior to Gwen's. These days, the two are more evenly matched. Charmcaster draws her weapons from a magical bag of tricks. That small bag stores some im-

ZOMBOZO

possibly large items, including a long magic staff that used to belong to her uncle Hex, another villain.

He may look big and bad, but Vulkanus is actually a small Detrovite alien who wears enhanced armor. In battle, he relies on his artificial strength and an arsenal of alien weapons. He could be really dangerous if there was some artificial intelligence under that armor, too.

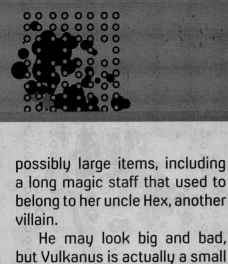

CHARMCASTER

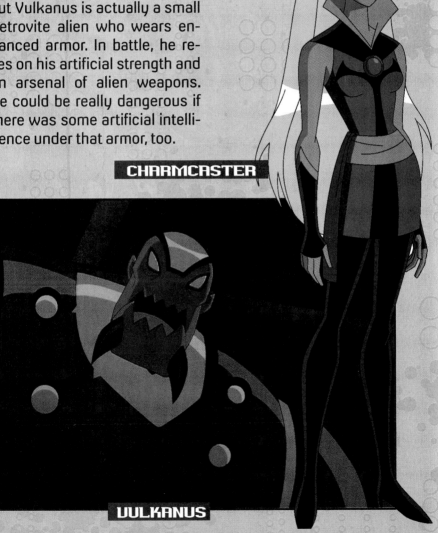

VULKANUS

SSSERPENT

"I am Ssserpent, the snake that walks like a man."

Those are the first words this villain uttered to Ben in his form as Cannonbolt — just before Cannonbolt flattened him like roadkill. Ssserpent served his time and got out on parole — only to break it by returning to Earth to commit some more crimes.

Unfortunately, Ssserpent didn't have any new tricks up his sssleeve. This time, Ben transformed into Four Arms. The two engaged in hand-to-hand-to-hand-to-hand combat. In the end, Four Arms prevailed, and Ssserpent sssurrendered.

WILL HARANGUE

When this sharp-tongued talk show host saw Ben's aliens forms on the Internet, he saw ratings gold. He used his power to make Ben public enemy number one, making him out to be an alien menace dangerous to Earth.

At first, Ben tried not to let Harangue's lies bother him. But then Harangue took things to a whole new level. First, he tricked Ben into thinking a video game producer wanted to make a game based on Ben and his alien forms. He had Ben demonstrate all of his moves and recorded them using cameras and motion-capture scanning gear.

Now Harangue had a catalogue of all of Ben's fighting moves. Then he programmed the Stalker — a killer robot — to respond to every one of Ben's moves. Harangue sent the Stalker after Ben, convinced there was no way his robot could lose.

Harangue challenged Ben to a televised showdown with the Stalker. Luckily, Ben remembered there was one alien form that didn't get scanned for the videogame — Nanomech. The tiny titan took down Harangue's giant robot. Harangue may have lost the fight — but he won the killer ratings he was looking for.

PSYPHON

Uilgax, Ben's greatest enemy, has tried many times to steal the Omnitrix. His lackey Psyphon was almost always by his side, but never in the driver's seat.

But when Vilgax was defeated for the last time, Psyphon returned to Earth to seek revenge for his master. He proved to be a formidable foe. The crackling energy blasts he shot from his hands were able to take down Gwen's energy shields. He also got some help from his three Robotic Extermination Devices, the REDs.

Ben transformed into Spidermonkey and then Ultimate Spidermonkey to try to take down Psyphon, but Psyphon knocked him out. When Ben came to, Psyphon was defeated. He thought Ultimate Spidermonkey had done it with a final punch, but it was actually JT and Cash who drained the villain's power with an alien weapon.

Ben has had several encounters with Dr. Animo. This villain started out as a respected researcher in animal medicine. Then the mad doctor began performing twisted experiments, trying to turn animals into monsters that would do his bidding.

Dr. Animo's latest experiments involved a yeti, a creature thought to be a mythical beast. The yeti is a half-human, half-ape creature with white fur and is sometimes called the Abominable Snowman. Dr. Animo used mind control to order a yeti to attack Ben.

Ben transformed into Four Arms to fight the beast, while Dr. Animo planned to unleash his Devolution Bomb on the world. When the bomb was activated, anyone within range would be transformed into a yeti. Ben wasn't thrilled with the idea of becoming a snow monster, so he transformed into Brain Storm. With his new super brain-power, he took control of the yeti and turned it on Dr. Animo.

GLOSSARY

ANODITE: A being from the planet Anodyne. Anodites can manipulate living energy and are able to become pure energy beings.

BUGZAPPER: A device used to turn DNAliens back into humans.

DASYPODIDAE: This creature from the planet Turrawuste may be small, but it can mean big trouble. Dasypodidae attack in swarms and, like piranhas on Earth, they will tear apart prey in a furious feeding frenzy.

DEVOLUTION BOMB: Dr. Animo's weapon can turn anyone within range into a yeti, a half-man, half-ape, snow creature.

DRAVEC: This alien monster looks like a giant worm with a mouthful of sharp teeth. It lives under the sand and emerges to surprise its prey. It is native to the planet Turrawuste.

GALVAN PRIME: A scientifically advanced world. It is home to the scientist Azmuth, who created the Omnitrix.

HOLO-VIEWER: A small device capable of projecting a three-dimensional holographic image of the person sending a message.

HYPERDRIVE: A speed faster than the speed of light.

HYPERSPACE JUMP GATE: A device capable of opening up huge rifts in hyperspace that allow large warships to cross the galaxy in a matter of seconds.

KORMITE: A glowing rock found in the Null Void. It is a powerful fuel source.

LOS SOLEDAD: This abandoned military base was the site of Paradox's time travel experiments in the 1950s. Because the time portal malfunctioned, the fabric of reality here is very thin.

MAGISTER: A rank in the Plumbers. A magister is in charge of other Plumbers in several space quadrants.

MANNA: The life energy found in everything from aliens to humans to plants. Gwen can use manna to track down a living thing by following its energy trail.

MAP OF INFINITY: Azmuth calls this the most important object in the universe. It's a complete map of space-time, extending through seventeen dimensions. The owner of the map could travel anywhere in the universe — even to the Forge of Creation, where the universe began. Knowing how dangerous it could be in the wrong hands, Paradox divided it into four pieces and stored them in safe places around the universe.

MR. SMOOTHY: This fast-food joint is where Ben gets his favorite drink — smoothies. After Ben became famous, Mr. Smoothy named ten flavors after his alien forms.

NULL GUARDS: Created by the Galvans, these creatures are the faceless watchdogs of the Null Void. Their job is to keep inhabitants of the Null Void safe from the dangerous criminals there.

NULL VOID: An extradimensional prison for intergalactic criminals. It's where the Plumbers send the bad guys they catch. But not everyone in the Null Void is evil. The Galvans set up the Null Void as a penal colony. Over time, communities of families sprang up there. Then other species started using the Null Void as a criminal dumping ground.

NULL VOID PROJECTOR: Plumbers use this handheld device, which shoots out a beam. Whatever the beam hits gets sent directly into the Null Void.

OSMOSIAN: An alien species that is able to absorb matter, energy, or the powers of any living creature. Kevin and Aggregor are both Osmosian.

PLUMBERS: Members of an intergalactic police force.

PLUMBERS' BADGES: Round, glowing badges carried by Pumbers. The badges can be used to track the location of other Plumbers and send distress signals to other badges. Each badge contains a translation circuit that automatically translates alien language into the Plumber's native language.

PLUMBERS' SNAKE: An unbreakable pan-dimensional retrieval system. It's basically a long cable you can attach to something before sending it into the inescapable Null Void. To retrieve whatever you've sent in, just reel in the cable.

POWER DECOUPLER: A large alien gun that can draw energy out of anything, store it, and then convert it to other kinds of energy or mass.

SHOCK STAFF: Aggregor's weapon gives out a powerful energy charge that can be calibrated to penetrate any other energy field.

SUPERSONIC: A speed greater than the speed of sound

TAYDENITE: The rarest, most precious gem in the galaxy is also the strongest. Taydenite can drill through anything.

TECHNOPATH: Someone who is able to communicate with technology. Ben's friend Cooper is a technopath.

TELEPORTER POD: Who needs a flying saucer for space travel when you've got a teleporter pod? Step inside this handy device and you can be transported to one of the many pods located all over the universe.

TIME PORTAL: Created by the scientist known as Paradox. A device capable of sending the user backward or forward in time and space.

TURRAWUSTE: A desert planet. There's not much happening on Turrawuste. Its main use is as a relay station for intergalactic transport.

WRENCH: When Grandpa Max ended up in the Null Void, he found that the evil Dr. Animo had become the superpowerful D'Void, and taken control of the extradimensional prison world. Grandpa Max took on the identity of the Wrench and led the fight against D'Void.

XENOCITE: A slimy parasite that looks half lobster, half larvae. When it latches onto a human's face, the doomed human is transformed into a DNAlien.